Pictures by Susan Perl

New York ABINGDON PRESS *Nashville*

MARION CONGER

WHO HAS SEEN THE WIND?

Who has seen the wind?
Neither I nor you;
But when the leaves hang trembling
The wind is passing thro'.

Who has seen the wind?
Neither you nor I;
But when the trees bow down their heads
The wind is passing by.

Christina G. Rossetti

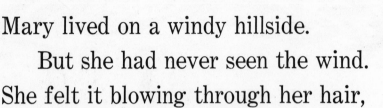

Mary lived on a windy hillside.
    But she had never seen the wind.
She felt it blowing through her hair,
    and she heard it talking in the trees
    on bright autumn days.
"Who? Who? Who?" it called as it
    sent dry leaves skipping over the lawn,
    and tossed red apples at Mary's feet,
    crisp and crunchy, good to eat.
"Who has seen me, Mary?"
    asked the autumn wind.
    "Who? Who? Who?"

"Have *you* seen the wind?"
Mary asked the milkman.
"No, I can't say that I have," said the milkman.
"But I can hear it all right.
It says that winter will be coming soon."
And, of course, winter did come.
And with it came clouds and snow and cold.
"Who? Who? Who?" called the wind as it
swept down from the north
and whistled round the corner of the house.

It nipped Mary's nose and
made her cheeks shine
like polished apples.
It shook the quiet snowflakes from the trees,
and they fell like stars on Mary's face.

It piled the snow into huge drifts
    that were just right for snow forts.
Inside her fort Mary couldn't feel the wind,
    but she could hear it passing overhead.
"Who, Mary? Who?" it roared.
    "Who? Who? Who?"

"Have *you* seen the wind?"
Mary asked the mailman.
"No, not me," grumbled the mailman.
"But I can feel it.
I can feel it all right!"
As he spoke, his breath made a frosty cloud.
And the wind picked up the cloud
and whisked it away.

One evening Mary and her father
sat by the fire popping corn.
"Listen to the wind!" said Mary.
It shook the windowpanes
and knocked at all the doors.
"Who? Who? Who?" it shouted as if
it were very angry indeed.
"I think the wind
is begging to come in," said Mary.
"It must be cold out there."

"But if we let it in," said Mary's father,
"It would soon blow out the fire.
And then it would be cold in here!"
"Have you seen the wind, Daddy?" asked Mary.
"Tell me about the wind."
"I have never seen the wind," he said.
"But I know how important it can be."

"It is important to those who fly in airplanes.
A tailwind gets behind an airplane
and speeds it on its way.
But a headwind pushes against an airplane
and slows the airplane down.
The wind is important to sailors, too.
A wind will fill their sails
and send their boats racing.
It sings through the rigging
and splashes spray in their faces.

But when there is no wind,
the sails hang limp and useless.
The sailboats cannot move.
The sailors are becalmed."
"Do airplane pilots and sailors see the wind?"
Mary asked.
"I don't know," said her father.
"I really don't know."

When spring came, the wind was warm,
and it played games with Mary.
Sometimes it brought rain.
And sometimes it brought the sun.
It was a teasing wind.

"Who? Who? Who?" it called as it
    tugged at Mary's kite string
    and lifted her kite
        into the wide blue sky.
Mary had to hold on tight
    to keep her kite
        from blowing away.

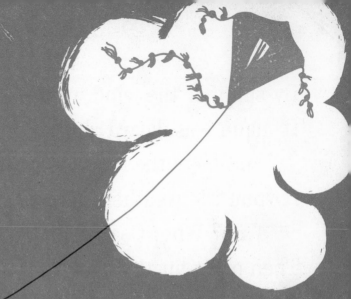

Once that wild spring wind lifted
    Mary's new straw hat right off her head!
Away across the yard sailed Mary's hat.
And away she ran to catch up with it.

By summer the wind was warm and joyous.
It made washboard ripples on the pond,
    and blew the flag out straight.
It spun the weathercock and called,
    "Who? Who? Cockadoodle doo?"
Then off it hustled leaving
        the weathercock still
        and the flag hanging limp and quiet.
But before Mary could wonder where it was,
        back it rushed to unfold the flag
            and billow it out again.
    "Who? Who? Hooray!" it seemed to say.
And all the laundry began to flap on the line
        as if the sheets and shirts and overalls
            thought they were flags, too.

Mary's mother threw open doors and windows
to let the wind blow through the house.
And with it came the smell of summer flowers.
"Have you seen the wind, Mother?" asked Mary.
"Sometimes I think I have," said Mary's mother.
"But I can never say for sure."
"Who *has* seen the wind?" asked Mary.
"You have asked the milkman," said her mother.
"And you have asked the mailman,
and you have asked Daddy,
and you have asked me.
Why don't you ask the wind?"

Mary went into the yard.
　　She lay down on her back
　　　　in the soft, clovery grass.
　　And the wind came close around,
　　　　ruffling her hair.
"Who has seen you, wind?" asked Mary.
　　"Who?　Who?　Who?"

The wind brushed Mary's cheeks
as if it were kissing her.
And it answered very softly,
"You. You. You."

"Mother," called Mary, running into the house.

"Mother, I know who has seen the wind!"

"Who has?" asked her mother.

"I have," said Mary.

"The wind told me, and of course it's true.

I have seen it in the trees,

and the grass,

and the snowflakes,

and the ripples on the pond.

I have seen it in the flag,

and the weathercock,

and the clothes on the clothesline.

Why I see it every day, don't I, Mother?"

And the wind answered,
"You do.
You do.
You do!"

3541